SCOTTISH
FAIRY TALES

SCOTTISH
FAIRY TALES

RETOLD BY PHILIP WILSON

Illustrated by
Sue Clarke, Anna Cynthia Leplar, Jacqueline Mair,
Sheila Moxley, and Jane Tattersfield

Contents

The Sprightly Tailor

Long ago, in a castle called Sandell, lived a laird called the great MacDonald. MacDonald liked his comfort, and favoured garments called trews, which were a combination of vest and trousers in one piece. One day the laird needed some new trews, and called for the local tailor.

When the tailor arrived the great MacDonald told him what he wanted. "I'll pay you extra," promised the laird, "if you will make the trews in the church by night." For MacDonald had heard that the church was haunted by a fearful monster, and he

wanted to see how the tailor fared when faced with this beast.

The tailor had also heard stories about the monster. But he was a sprightly fellow who liked a challenge – especially if it was going to lead to some extra money. So that very night he walked up the glen, through the churchyard gate, and into

the dark church. Finding a
tombstone where he could sit,
he got to work on the trews,
and very soon the garment was
taking shape.

After a while, the tailor felt
the floor of the church begin
to shake beneath him. A hole
seemed to open up in the
stone floor and a large and
gruesome head appeared. "Do
you see this great head of mine?" a voice boomed.

"I see that, but I'll sew these," replied the tailor, holding up
the trews.

The head paused as the tailor was speaking, then began to
rise again, revealing a thick, muscular neck. "Do you see this
great neck of mine?" the monster asked.

"I see that, but I'll sew these," replied the tailor.

Next the creature's shoulders and trunk came into view. "Do
you see this great chest of mine?"

"I see that, but I'll sew these," said the tailor. And he carried
on sewing, although, to tell the truth, some of the stitches were
a little less neat than normal.

Now the beast was rising quickly, and the tailor could make

out its arms. Its voice echoed in the stone building: "Do you see these great arms of mine?"

"I see those, but I'll sew these," replied the tailor. He gritted his teeth and carried on with his work as before, for he wanted to finish by daybreak and claim his payment from the great MacDonald.

The tailor's needle was flying now, as the monster gave a great grunt and lifted his first leg out of the ground. "Do you see this great leg of mine?" he said, his voice getting even louder.

"I see that, but I'll sew these," replied the tailor, making his final stitches a little longer, so that he could finish his work before the monster could climb out of his hole.

As the creature began to raise its other leg, the tailor blew out his candle, gathered up his things, and bundled the completed trews under one arm. He made for the door as the monster was emerging, and the tailor could hear the creature's footsteps echoing on the stone floor as he ran out into the open air.

Now the tailor could see the glen stretching in front of him, and he ran for his life, faster than he had ever ran before, for all that he was a nimble man. The monster roared at him to stop, but the tailor hurried on, his feet hardly touching the ground, and finally the great MacDonald's castle loomed up ahead of him and the tailor knew he had a chance to reach its gates.

Quickly the gates opened, and quickly they closed behind the tailor – and not a moment too soon, for as the great wooden gates slammed shut, the monster crashed to a halt and struck a resounding blow on the wall to show how frustrated he was at missing his goal when he had got so near.

To this day, the monster's handprint can be seen on the wall of the castle at Sandell. MacDonald paid the sprightly tailor for his work, and gave him a handsome bonus for braving the haunted church. The laird liked his smart new trews, and never realised that some of the stitches were longer and less neat than the others.

Gold-Tree and Silver-Tree

There once lived a king who had a queen called Silver-Tree and a beautiful daughter called Gold-Tree. They all lived together happily until one day Silver-Tree and Gold-Tree were sitting by a pool and it took Silver-Tree's fancy to peer into the water and talk to the trout swimming there: "Silver trout in the pool, who is the most beautiful queen in the world?"

"Gold-Tree is the most beautiful," replied the fish.

Silver-Tree was mad with jealousy. She could not stand the fact that there was someone in the world – someone in her very family – who was more beautiful than she. She decided that she would get Gold-Tree killed, and to be sure the girl was dead, she would eat Gold-Tree's heart and liver. The queen was so mad with jealousy that she told her husband, begging him to kill their daughter and give her the heart and liver to eat.

At just this time it happened that a prince from a far country had come to ask for Gold-Tree's hand in marriage. The king, who was a good man, saw that the two young people loved each other, and saw his chance. He sent Gold-Tree away with the prince to be married. Then, when out hunting with his

men, he took a deer's heart and liver, and gave them to his wife. Once she had eaten these, Silver-Tree was cured of her jealousy.

All went well until the queen visited the pool and again asked the fish who was the most beautiful.

"Gold-Tree your daughter is the fairest," said the trout.

"But my daughter is long dead!" exclaimed the queen.

"Surely she is not. For she has married a fine prince in a far country."

When Silver-Tree asked her husband she found that what

the trout had said was true.

"Make ready the great ship, for I must visit my daughter," said Silver-Tree. And because she had seemed cured of her jealousy, the king let her go.

When Silver-Tree came to her destination, the prince was out hunting. Gold-Tree saw her mother arriving, and knew that her life was in danger. She called her servants, and they locked Gold-Tree in her room. But Silver-Tree was cunning. When she found her daughter locked in, she called sweetly, "Put your little finger through the keyhole, so your mother may kiss it."

As soon as Gold-Tree's finger appeared through the keyhole, the wicked queen took a dagger that she had dipped in poison and stuck it into Gold-Tree's finger. Straight away, the princess collapsed, and soon she was dead, the poisoned point still in her finger as she lay.

When Gold-Tree's husband came home, he was horrified at what had happened. He broke into the room and saw his young wife dead on the floor. So beautiful was the dead princess, that he had her body preserved, and locked in her room, and kept the key himself.

After some years had passed, the prince's grief faded a little, although he never smiled, and he decided to marry once again. He did not tell his second wife about Gold-Tree's body, but one day she found the key to the dead girl's room. She was curious to see the one part of her husband's castle that she had never entered, so, when no one was looking, she quietly opened the door and went in. When she saw the beautiful body laid out in the room, she realised at once that this must be Gold-Tree, the princess who had died so tragically, for she had heard the tale of the girl's death. As she approached the body she saw the poisoned dagger still sticking in the girl's finger. Yes, this must be Gold-Tree. Still curious, the second wife pulled at the dagger to remove it, and Gold-Tree rose, alive, just as she had been before her mother's visit.

The second wife went to the prince and said to him, "What would you give me if I could make you laugh again?"

"Truly, nothing could make me laugh, unless Gold-Tree was alive again," said the prince sadly.

"Then come to her room, and surely you will find her living."

They ran to the room together and the prince saw that it was true. The second wife was amazed at the change that came over her husband and knew that Gold-Tree was his true love.

"Now you have your true love back again," she said, "I must go away."

But the prince was so grateful to her that he would not let her go. He insisted that she remain in his household, alongside Gold-Tree.

Everything went well for them until Silver-Tree visited the pool once more. The queen was horrified when the fish told her that Gold-Tree was still the most beautiful woman in the world.

"But I stabbed Gold-Tree with poison and she is long dead," protested the queen.

"You stabbed her, but she is still alive," the fish replied.

And so Silver-Tree once more set sail to her daughter's home, and it happened that the prince was out hunting when she arrived. Gold-Tree saw her mother approaching, and quaked with fear at what she would do. "Let us go to meet her," said the second wife calmly, and they went together, as if to greet a welcome guest.

Silver-Tree held out a precious gold cup that she was carrying. "I bring a refreshing drink for my daughter," she said.

The second wife looked at her coldly. "In this country, it is the custom for the visitor to drink first," she said.

Silver-Tree raised the cup to her mouth, but hesitated, knowing that if she drank, she would kill herself. Just at that moment, the second wife's arm shot out and struck the cup, sending some of the deadly poison straight down Silver-Tree's throat. The wicked queen fell dead to the floor, and the servants took up her body to bury her. At last, Gold-Tree, the prince, and his second wife could live in peace.

The Black Bull of Norway

Long ago in Norway there lived a woman, and she had three daughters. One day the eldest daughter went to her mother and said that she had decided to seek her fortune. So the girl went to see the old witch-washerwoman who could foretell people's futures. And the witch-washerwoman said to her, "Stand by my back door and see what you can see."

The first day, the girl could see nothing unusual outside the witch-washerwoman's back door, and nothing came on the second day. But on the third day, a fine coach pulled by six

horses appeared in the road beyond the back door. The girl went to the witch-washerwoman and told her what she had seen. "That's for you," said the witch-washerwoman, and the girl got into the coach and rode away.

Soon the second daughter decided she too should seek her fortune, and went to the witch-washerwoman's house, as her sister had done. The first day, she could see nothing unusual outside the witch-washerwoman's back door, and nothing came on the second day. But on the third day, a fine coach appeared. "That's for you," said the witch-washerwoman, and the second daughter rode away.

Then the youngest daughter followed in her sisters' footsteps, going to the witch-washerwoman's house in her turn. The first

day, she could see nothing outside the witch-washerwoman's back door, and nothing came on the second day. But on the third day, a great black bull appeared, bellowing as it walked. "That's for you," said the witch-washerwoman.

The girl was fearful of the great black creature, but in the end she plucked up the courage to climb on to the beast's back, and they galloped away together. The bull seemed kind, and when the girl felt hungry and asked for refreshment, the bull said, "Eat from out my right ear, and take drink from my left." The girl did so, and felt wonderfully refreshed.

By and by they came to a fine castle, and the bull slowed down at its gate. "Here lives my eldest brother," said the bull, and the two rested for the night at the castle. In the morning, the lord of the castle took the girl into a fine chamber, and gave her an apple. "Do not break into this apple until you are in the greatest need," said the lord. "Then it will help you."

The girl and the bull rode on for many miles more, until they arrived at a second castle, bigger and fairer than the first. "Here lives my second brother," said the bull, and the two rested there for the night.

In the morning, the lord of the castle took the girl into a fine chamber, and presented her with a pear. And he spoke to her rather as the first lord had done. "Do not break into this pear until you are in need," said the lord. "Then it will help you."

Once again the two travelled on, over hill and dale, until they came to a third castle, still finer and larger than the others. "Here lives my youngest brother," said the bull, and the lord of the castle once more gave them lodgings for the night.

In the morning, the lord of the castle took the girl into a fine chamber, and presented her with a plum. "Do not break into this fruit until you are in the greatest need," said the lord. "Then it will help you."

Off they went again, and after another long ride, the bull came to a halt in a dark and lonely glen. "This is where you

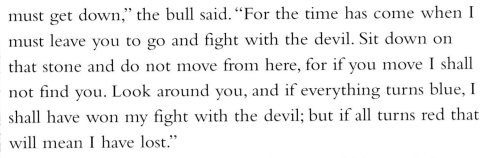

must get down," the bull said. "For the time has come when I must leave you to go and fight with the devil. Sit down on that stone and do not move from here, for if you move I shall not find you. Look around you, and if everything turns blue, I shall have won my fight with the devil; but if all turns red that will mean I have lost."

After a while everything in the glen turned blue, and the girl's heart was filled with joy that the bull had won his fight. So pleased she was that she moved one foot and crossed it over the other, quite forgetting the bull's instructions to stay absolutely still. So, no matter how long she sat, the bull could not find her again.

When the black bull did not return, the girl saw the reason, and she knew that she must complete her journey alone. So off she went along the glen, until she came to a great hill made all of glass. She walked around the hill, but could not climb it, for its glassy surface was so slippery. Finally she found a smith's house, and the smith told her that he would make her some metal shoes so that she could cross the hill in safety.

The girl climbed the glassy hill, and made her way carefully down the other side, and what should she see but the house of the old witch-washerwoman – her journey had brought her full circle. When she was talking to the washerwoman and her daughter, they told her of a handsome knight who had

brought some blood-stained shirts
to be washed. The blood had
almost ruined the shirts, so he had
promised to marry the woman
who could wash away the stains,
but neither the old washerwoman
nor her daughter could do this,
no matter how they rubbed and
scrubbed.

The girl took the shirts and
began to wash them, and both the
washerwoman and her daughter
turned green with envy as they
saw the bloodstains
disappearing. But when the
knight returned for his shirts,
the washerwoman told him
that it was her daughter who
had washed them. And so it
happened that the knight and
the washerwoman's daughter
prepared to get married.

The girl wondered what to
do, since she admired the

knight and desperately wanted the truth to be known. So she decided to break open the apple she had been given at the first castle. Out tumbled a heap of gold and jewels. "Delay your marriage for one day," said the girl to the washerwoman's daughter, "and you shall have these jewels."

The bride-to-be agreed, and the girl planned to go to the knight in the evening and explain the truth to him. But the washerwoman saw how things stood and gave the knight a sleeping-potion to drink. Through her tears, the girl sang a snatch of song:

The bloody shirt I washed for thee.
Will you not waken and turn to me?

Next day, the girl could think of nothing to do but break open her pear. Out came jewels even more precious than those that had come out of the apple. "Delay your marriage for one day," said the girl to the washerwoman's daughter, "and you shall have them all."

The washerwoman's daughter agreed, and the girl once more got ready to go to the knight. But once again the washerwoman gave him a sleeping-potion, so that the truth could not be told him. Again the girl sang through her tears of sadness:

> The bloody shirt I washed for thee.
> Will you not waken and turn to me?

The knight heard nothing of this song. But the next day, when he was out hunting, one of his men said to him, "What was that singing and moaning last night outside your chamber?" The knight, curious to find out what was going on, was determined that nothing should make him fall asleep the next night.

Meanwhile, the girl broke open the plum, and still richer jewels fell out. These she offered to the washerwoman's girl, who again accepted them. But this time, the knight, who by now suspected the washerwoman, only pretended to drink.

So it was that the knight came to hear the truth. The girl who had ridden the black bull, climbed the hill of glass, and washed the blood-stained shirt finally married her knight. And the washerwoman's daughter was content with her jewels.

The Well at the World's End

There was once a king, a widower, and he had a daughter who was beautiful and good-natured. The king married a queen, who was a widow, and she had a daughter who was as ugly and ill-natured as the king's daughter was fair and good. The queen detested the king's daughter, for no one would notice her own girl while this paragon was beside her, so she made a plan. She sent the king's daughter to the well at the world's end, with a bottle to get some water, thinking she would never come back.

The girl walked far and was beginning to tire when she came upon a pony tethered by the roadside. The pony looked at the girl and spoke: "Ride me, ride me, fair princess."

"Yes, I will ride you," replied the girl, and the pony carried her over a moor covered with prickly gorse and brambles.

Far she rode, and finally she came to the well at the world's end. She took her bottle and lowered it into the well, but the well was too deep and she could not fill the bottle. Then three old men came up to her, saying, "Wash us, wash us, fair maid, and dry us with your linen apron."

So she washed the men and in return they lowered her bottle into the well and filled it with water.

When they had finished, the three men looked at the girl and spoke her future. "If she was fair before, she will be ten times more beautiful," said the first.

"A diamond and a ruby and a pearl shall drop from her mouth every time she speaks," predicted the second.

"Gold and silver shall come from her hair when she combs it," said the third.

The king's daughter returned to court, and to everyone's amazement, these predictions came true.

All were happy with the girl's good fortune, except for the

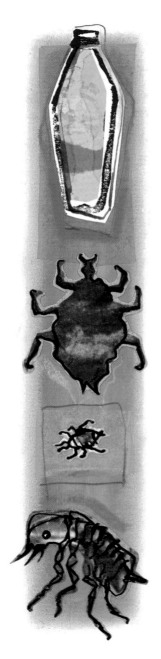

queen and her daughter. The queen decided that she would send her own daughter to the well at the world's end, to get her the same gifts. After travelling far, the girl came to the pony, as the king's daughter had done before her. By now, the beast was tethered once more. But when the creature asked her to ride it, the queen's daughter replied, "Don't you see I am a queen's daughter? I will not ride you, you filthy beast."

The proud girl walked on, and she soon came to the moor covered with gorse and brambles. It was hard going for the girl, and the thorns cut her feet badly. Soon she could hardly walk with the pain.

After a long and painful walk across the moor, the queen's daughter came to the well at the world's end. She lowered her bottle, but like the king's daughter, found that it would not reach the water in the well. Then she heard the three old men speaking: "Wash us, wash us, fair maid, and dry us with your linen apron."

And the proud daughter replied, "You

26

nasty, filthy creatures, do you think a queen's daughter can be bothered to wash you, and dry your dirty faces with my fine clean clothes?"

So the old men refused to dip the girl's bottle into the well. Instead, they turned to her and began to predict her future: "If she was ugly before, she will be ten times uglier," said the first.

"Each time she speaks, a frog and a toad will jump from her mouth," predicted the second.

"When she combs her hair, lice and fleas will appear," said the third.

With these curses ringing in her ears, the unhappy girl returned home. Her mother was distraught when she saw her daughter, for she was indeed uglier than before, and frogs, toads, fleas, and lice, jumped from her. In the end, she left the king's court, and married a poor cobbler. The king's fair and good-natured daughter married a handsome prince, and was happy – and good-natured – for the rest of her long life.

27

The Princess of the Blue Mountains

There was a poor widow who had one son called Will.
Because he was all she had in the world she always let him
have his way, and he became lazy. In the end she said to him,
"Son, you must make your own way in the world. Then you
will know what it is to find your own work and earn your
own living." So young Will went off to seek his fortune.

Will travelled until he came to a fast-flowing river, which he
had to cross. When he saw the rapid current and the sharp
rocks, he was afraid to go into the water, and waited for a
while. As he was standing there, a lady on the opposite bank
saw him, and waved at him to cross, which finally he did.

When Will got to the other side, the lady said she would give
him food and drink if he would go into her garden and find
the most beautiful flower. But Will, struck by the lady's beauty,
said "You are the fairest flower in all the garden."

The lady, already charmed by Will, turned to him. "Will you
be my husband?" she asked. "There will be many dangers in
store for you, but I'll try to help you through them."

Will looked at the lady and it did not take him long to say "Yes, I will be your husband, whatever dangers I must face."

Then the lady explained her story to Will. She was the Princess of the Kingdom of the Blue Mountains, and had been stolen away from her father's land by a demon called Grimaldin. For three nights, the demon would send his legions to do battle with Will. The lady gave Will three black sticks, one for each legion of demons, and a pot of ointment, in case he should be injured. "Use these things well, for now I must leave you."

As soon as the lady had left, three legions of demons appeared. They were armed with fearsome clubs, which they

raised to beat Will. But the young man stopped their blows, and used the lady's sticks to beat them off. Soon they were gone.

The next morning, the lady returned, and was pleased to see Will hale and hearty. "Well done. Never before has any man fought off the demons with such skill and courage. Tonight, twice as many demons will come to challenge you, so I will give you six sticks to help you fight them off." And the lady left once more, this time giving Will a larger pot of ointment, in case he should be wounded.

Sure enough, six legions of demons arrived to do battle with Will and again he beat them off successfully.

The lady greeted Will with gladness the following morning. "This time, I must give you twelve sticks, for twelve legions will come tonight. Look out of Grimaldin, for he will certainly come too." She left more ointment, for no one had survived a fight with Grimaldin without being sorely wounded.

Quickly Grimaldin and his whole army of twelve legions arrived, and the chief demon spoke to Will: "What is your business here?"

"I come to rescue the Princess of the Blue Mountains."

"Then you shall die."

Straight away, the demons attacked, and Will beat them off with the sticks as before. But this time, Grimaldin attacked, and

struck Will to the ground. The young man, sore and wounded
all over, quickly applied the ointment. He was amazed to feel
whole and well again, and stood up to face Grimaldin. This
time, he beat off the chief demon, who went away, howling.

When the princess reappeared, she looked relieved. "Your
greatest danger is over," she said to Will. "Take this book about
the history of my family, and let no one distract you from
reading it. If you know all that is in this book, you will be one
of my father's favourites, and he will allow you to marry me."

Will started to read the book. He heard all sorts of voices trying to distract him, but he kept his eyes glued to the pages.
Then he heard a woman coming by selling apples. Will liked
nothing more than a ripe apple, so he looked up from the

book. No sooner had he done so than he felt himself thrown against the apple woman's basket with such force that he passed out.

A while later, Will came to. The apple woman was gone and the princess was nowhere to be seen. There was an old man sitting nearby on a bench and Will asked him if he knew how to get to the kingdom of the Blue Mountains. The old man did not know, so he asked the fishes of the sea, and no fish knew the whereabouts of the kingdom. The old man said "I have a brother, five hundred years older than me, who can talk to the birds of the air. He will know, or will find out from the birds."

They went to see the old

man's aged brother, and all the birds were called together. None knew where the kingdom of the Blue Mountains could be found, until the last bird, a great eagle, arrived. "I can take you to the kingdom," said the eagle. And Will climbed onto the great bird's back.

In the kingdom of the Blue Mountains, they landed near a house hung with black drapery. Will asked for lodgings, but the people at the house said that they could not help him. Their master was to be fed to a giant who terrorized the kingdom, asking for a human victim to eat every day. Anyone who could kill the giant would please the king, and would be given the hand of his daughter in marriage.

Will knew what he must do. He put on his armour, and strode out to challenge the giant. They fought long and hard, and Will was finally the winner. The princess recognized him and when the king learned that he had killed the giant, gave his permission for Will and the princess to marry. After the wedding, Will's mother came to live with them at the royal castle, and they were all happy together.

The Widow's Son and the King's Daughter

There was once a young lad called Jack, whose father died, leaving Jack and his mother without money. So, for the first time in his life, Jack had to go out to work. He had few useful skills, but he knew that he was no use to his mother at home, so set off one day to seek his fortune, whatever it might be.

After travelling a long way on the first day, Jack came across a house near a wood. He stopped and talked to the people of the house and, as he looked weak from his journey, they offered him food and a bed for the night. In the morning, the man of the house asked Jack if he needed work, and Jack replied that he did. "I have a herd of cattle that needs minding," said the man. "If you will do that job for me I should be pleased. But do not go into the field with the fruit trees. For a giant lives in that field and he will surely gobble you up if you go there. He may even carry off my cattle to eat."

Jack went to the field to mind the cattle, and he had not been there long when he started to admire the fruit on the trees in the neighbouring field. There were red apples and ripe pears, as well as all sorts of other strange fruit that Jack did not recognise. He peered through the hedge and no one seemed to be about. So Jack thought he would risk a quick dash into the giant's field to take some fruit.

As Jack was picking some of the fruit, an old woman passed along the lane that ran by the edge of the field. She was also admiring the fruit, and asked Jack if he would pick some for her. Looking around him cautiously to make sure the giant was not coming, Jack agreed, and soon both he and the old woman had some fine, succulent fruit to eat.

"I will give you something useful in return for your favour," the old woman said to Jack. "Here are three stout rods and a

sword. Whoever you stab with this sword, they will be sure to fall down dead. You need never fear your enemies."

Jack thanked the old woman with all his heart, for in truth he had been worried about the giant, and wondered whether the beast would stride over the hedge into his field and take his revenge for the stolen fruit.

Sure enough, it was not long before the giant appeared. Jack hastily climbed a tree, for he had not tried the sword and wondered whether it would work. This did not put off the giant, who stepped towards the tree, held out his hand, and heaved. The tree was torn up by the roots, and Jack fell to the ground. But as the giant did this, Jack's sword grazed his flesh, and the giant fell down dead.

The next day, Jack was guarding his master's cattle again, when another giant appeared by the trees. "Do you dare to slay my brother?" the beast bellowed. Jack drew his sword and ran at the giant, felling the beast with one blow. As he looked at the massive corpse, Jack wondered if there were any more in the giant's family.

On the third day, another giant appeared. Jack hid himself in the hollow of a tree, and heard the creature grunting that he must have one of Jack's beasts to eat. "You will have to ask me first," shouted Jack from inside the hollow tree.

"Oh, is it you, who killed my two brothers?" roared the giant. "I shall take my revenge on you before long." But as the giant drew near the tree, Jack leaped out and stabbed him. The last of the giants was dead.

When he had got his breath back, Jack decided to go to the giants' castle, which was not far off, and see what riches might be hidden there. When he arrived, he told the giant's steward, who looked after the castle, that he had conquered the giants, and the steward, amazed at Jack's strength, gave the lad the keys to the castle treasuries. Jack took some of the money he found there and travelled back home to see his own people.

Jack found his country in turmoil when he arrived. People were weeping, and they told him that a fire-breathing monster had come to the country and had demanded one young boy or girl to eat every day. Tomorrow, it was the turn of the king's daughter, who would be killed by the beast if no one could slay the monster or drive it away.

Jack put on his armour and took his faithful sword. Then he went to see the princess whom the monster was hoping to devour. He told her that he had come to save her, and asked if she would marry him if he was successful. To this she agreed, and in relief, Jack fell at her feet and was soon asleep with his head in the princess's lap. While Jack was asleep, the princess wove a ringlet of white stones in his hair, as a good-luck charm.

Suddenly, the monster crashed into the room. The princess started in fear and Jack woke up. In one movement he jumped up and drew his sword. Holding the weapon in front of him, he aimed many blows at the monster, but he could not get close enough to wound the beast because of the fire that came spurting from the creature's mouth. They carried on like this for some time, Jack waving his sword and the beast spitting fire, until the monster began to tire and slunk away.

The next day, the beast returned. The same thing happened,

with neither the beast nor Jack the winner, until the monster again grew tired and this time flapped its wings and flew away.

Jack thought hard. It was the creature's fire that caused the problem. So on the third day, Jack borrowed a camel, and made the animal drink several barrels of water. When the dragon appeared, Jack made the camel spit out its water to put out the fire. Then, before the monster could produce more flames, Jack went in for the kill, stabbing the beast and laying it low. At last the princess, and all her people, were saved.

Jack and the princess were betrothed, and Jack went away for some more adventures before his planned wedding day. After

nine months, the
princess had a baby, but
no one knew who the
father could be. The
king was angry with
his daughter, but she
persuaded him to go
with her to see a fairy,
who might be able to
give them the answer.
The fairy placed a
lemon in the child's
hand and said, "Only
the child's true father
will be able to take this
fruit from its hand."

The king then called
all the men in his
kingdom to the palace
and every one of them
tried to take away the
lemon. But no matter
how hard they tried,
the fruit would not

come away from the baby's hand. Finally, Jack appeared, and as soon as he touched the baby, the lemon came away.

The king was filled with anger towards Jack and his daughter, and wanted them to leave the palace forthwith. So he put the princess and Jack in rags and set them in a rotten boat and cast them out to sea. Just as the couple thought that they were going to sink, a lady appeared. "I was the fairy who gave Jack his sword, and the one who protected the princess from the breath of the beast," she said. "Once more, I will help you." She repaired the boat, turned their rags to fine robes, and so they returned to the palace.

Now Jack explained to the king who he was. "I was the man who saved your daughter from becoming the victim of the monster," said Jack. And Jack produced the king's gold cup, which he had taken before, and the monster's head, to show he spoke true. As further proof, the princess showed them all the ringlet of stones in Jack's hair. Convinced of the truth, the king allowed the couple to marry. They lived in happiness, and eventually, Jack himself became king.

Kate Crackernuts

Long ago there lived a king and a queen and each had a daughter. The king's daughter, Kate, was fairer than the queen's daughter, and the queen grew jealous of her. Soon the queen was plotting to find a way to spoil Kate's beauty.

The queen went to see a witch, who asked her to keep Kate from her food and to send the girl to her. So the next morning the queen sent Kate to the witch, to ask for some eggs. But Kate managed to snatch a bite to eat before she left the house. When Kate arrived, the witch said, "Lift the lid off that pot over there," and Kate obeyed. But nothing happened. "Tell your mother to keep the larder locked," said the witch.

So the queen knew that Kate had had something to eat, and was more careful on the next morning. Again Kate went to the witch, but on her way she saw some country people picking peas. They gave the hungry girl some peas to eat, so once more nothing happened when the witch asked Kate to open the pot.

On the third day the queen herself went with Kate to the witch, watching the girl all the way. When Kate lifted the lid of the pot, out popped the head of a sheep, and this instantly changed places

with Kate's own head. The
queen was satisfied at last.

When the queen's daughter
saw Kate, she was sorry for
her half-sister. So she put a
cloth over Kate's head and
announced: "Let us go and
seek our fortunes, and see if
anyone in the world can cure
you." The two girls travelled
far until they came to a great
castle. Kate's sister did not feel
well, so they hoped to find
lodgings in the castle. When
they asked some passers-by,
they found that it belonged
to a king. They knocked on
the door, and the guards let
them in.

Once inside the castle
courtyard, the girls told the
people they were travellers far
away from home and asked if
they could have lodgings for

the night. They were soon granted their wish, as long as Kate would stay up at night to look after the king's sick son. A purse of silver was promised to Kate if she did this, and she readily agreed.

All went well until midnight. As the castle clock struck twelve, the prince began to climb out of bed. He put on his clothes, opened the door of his room, and went downstairs to the stables. Kate followed, but made sure that the prince did not see him, even when she jumped silently up on the horse behind him.

Off they rode through a forest, and as they went, Kate reached up into the trees and picked nuts from the branches, gathering them all in her apron. When they reached a green hill, the prince stopped his horse. "Open and let the prince enter," said the king's son. "And his lady too," said Kate, quietly.

One side of the green hill opened and they rode in. Kate saw

a fine hall, filled with lords and ladies who were dancing. Kate sat by the door, where she saw some fairies and a child playing with a wand. "Three strokes of the wand would make Kate's sister well," said one of the fairies. So Kate rolled nuts across the floor to the child until he forgot the wand, and Kate hid it in her apron.

Then a cock crew, the prince mounted his horse, and Kate jumped up behind. Together they rode back to the castle. As soon as she could, Kate tapped her sister three times with the fairy wand, bringing her back to health. Kate's sister then touched Kate with the wand. The sheep's head disappeared, and Kate's fair face returned. Then Kate sat by the fire, cracking her nuts, and eating them, as if nothing had happened. When the king asked her how she had fared with his son, she replied that he had had a good night. The king asked her to sit with him one night more, and he offered her a purse of gold

pieces in payment if she would.

So the next night saw Kate once more sitting by the prince's bedside, and, when the clock struck midnight, the prince went to his horse and rode again to the green hill, as before.

The king asked Kate to watch his son for one night more. "How shall I reward you this time?" asked the king.

"Let me marry your son if I look after him for a third night."

As on the two previous nights, the prince went to his horse at midnight and rode to the green hill. Kate sat quietly as the prince danced. Once more, she noticed the small child who had had the wand. This time, he was playing with a bird, and Kate heard one of the fairies say, "Three bites of that bird would cure the prince." So Kate rolled nuts across the floor to the child until he forgot the bird, and Kate hid it in her apron.

They returned to the castle, and instead of cracking her nuts as before, Kate plucked the bird and roasted it. When he smelled the bird, the prince said "That smells very fine. I would like to have some of that meat to eat." Kate gave him one bite, and the prince rose up, supporting his weight on his elbow; she gave him a second bite, and he sat up in bed; she gave him a third bite and he got up, and sat by the fire.

When the king and the others came into the room they found the prince and Kate cracking nuts and eating them together. The prince looked as well as could be, and soon they were married. Meanwhile, the king's other son married the queen's daughter. They all lived in happiness, and were never again troubled by royal jealousy.

The Son of the King of Ireland

One day the son of the King of Ireland was out hunting, and brought down a raven. He looked at the bird's black feathers and red blood, and he said to himself, "I will not marry until I find a woman with hair as black as the raven's feathers, and cheeks as red as the raven's blood."

When he got home he told his father, who replied, "You will not easily find such a woman."

The youth said, "I will travel the world until I find her."

So the son of the King of Ireland set off on his search. Everywhere he went, he asked people if they had seen a woman with hair as black as the raven's feathers, and cheeks as red as the raven's blood. And he was told that the King of the Great World had three daughters, and that the youngest was just such a woman. So the lad determined to find her.

On his way, the lad called on a smith, who was making a great needle. "You are in luck," said the smith. "This needle I am making is for the King of the Great World himself. His boat comes tomorrow to collect it, and I will ask his men to ferry you across to his castle."

In the morning the boat came and the lad jumped on board. When they arrived at the castle, the lad, dusty with travel as he was, went straight to the King of the Great World, to ask him for one of his daughters in marriage.

"If you want to marry my daughter, you must be of nobler birth than you look," said the king.

"I am the son of the King of Ireland," the boy replied.

The King of the Great World paused. "You shall win the hand of my daughter," he said. "But you must do three things. First, clear all the filth from my great barn, and make it so clean that a gold ball will run from one end of the floor to the other."

The youth began to clear the barn. But no matter how much

filth he removed, more came in its place. Just then, the king's three daughters came by. They could see that the lad was harassed and could not finish his task.

The eldest daughter said, "If I thought it was me you wanted, I would clear the barn for you." And the middle one said the same.

But the youngest daughter said, "Whether you have come for me or not, I will clear the barn." She said, "Clean, clean, pitchfork, put out shovel." Straight away the whole floor of the barn was clean.

When the king returned, he said he was pleased with the boy's work and told him his next task. "Tomorrow you must thatch the barn with birds' feathers. I want the stem of every feather to point inwards and whole roof to be secured with a silk thread."

As soon as the lad got any feathers on the roof, a wind came and blew them away. Then, the king's three daughters came by. The eldest said, "If I thought it was me you wanted, I would thatch the barn for you." And the middle one said the same.

But the youngest daughter said, "Whether you have come for me or not, I will thatch the barn." She took out her whistle and blew. Straightaway, a beautiful, neat thatch of birds' feathers covered the roof of the barn, just as the king had ordered.

When the king saw the barn he said, "I am pleased with your

work. But I am not pleased with your teacher. You have more work to do tomorrow. You must mind my five swans. If you let any of them escape, you will be hanged, but if you keep them, you shall have my daughter."

The boy tried to herd the swans together, but they always escaped. Then, the king's three daughters came by. The eldest said, "If I thought it was me you wanted, I would find the swans for you." And the middle one said the same.

But the youngest daughter said, "Whether you have come for me or not, I will find my father's swans." And she blew her whistle, and the swans came home.

When the King of the Great World arrived, the lad said, "Shall I get your daughter now?"

"Not yet," replied the king. "Tomorrow I am going fishing, and you must clean and cook the fish that I catch."

The next day the son of the King of Ireland began to scrape the scales from the fish. But no matter how many he removed, more appeared in their place. At that very moment, the king's three daughters came by. The eldest said, "If I thought it was me you wanted, I would clean the fish for you." And the middle one said the same.

But the youngest daughter said, "Whether you have come for me or not, son of the King of Ireland, I will clean the fish." And she cleaned the fish, saying, "My father will kill us both when he wakens. We must take flight together." And the pair

took flight, and galloped off together as fast as their steed could carry them.

Soon the king leapt on his horse, and gave chase. The lad and the princess heard the hooves of the king's horse beating on the ground behind them. The king's daughter said, "Look and see what you can find in the horse's ear."

"Just a little bit of thorn," said the lad.

"Throw it behind you," said the girl. At once, the thorn grew into a dense wood seven miles long. The king could not get through, until he called for an axe and hacked himself a path.

Again the daughter urged the lad, "Look in the horse's ear."

"A tiny stone," he said.

"Throw it behind you," she replied. And when he did, the stone turned into a massive rock, seven miles long and one mile high, and the couple were on the top.

The king could not climb the rock, so he returned home, and the couple went on their way to Ireland. As they approached the palace of the King of Ireland, the girl said, "I will not come in now. When you go in, the dog will jump up to welcome you. Try to keep him away, for if the dog touches your face, you will forget me."

So the couple went their separate ways. The daughter put on men's clothes and went to lodge with a smith who wanted a new apprentice. She stayed with him a year, and was soon the

best apprentice he had ever had.

Then a messenger arrived at the smithy, inviting the smith to the wedding of the son of the King of Ireland and the daughter of the King of Farafohuinn, and he decided to take his apprentice. "Please let me use the smithy tonight," said the daughter. By the following morning, she had made a hen of gold and a silver cockerel.

On the day of the wedding, the smith and his apprentice set off, she with the golden hen and silver cockerel, he with some grains of wheat in his pocket. Everyone was pleased to see them, and someone asked what they could do to entertain the guests. So the apprentice put the golden hen and the silver cockerel on the floor and threw down three grains of wheat. The cockerel picked up two grains, the hen only one.

"Do you remember how I cleaned the great barn for you? If you remembered, you would not take two grains instead of one," said the hen.

Everyone laughed, and they threw down another three grains. The same thing happened. "Do you remember when I thatched the barn with birds' feathers?" asked the hen.

As they threw down more grains, the son of the King of Ireland began to remember what had happened to him.

"Do you remember how I found the swans for you? If you remembered, you would not take two grains instead of one."

Now the king's son was sure. "It must be you," he shouted, and they undid the apprentice's costume to show that she was indeed a woman.

The son of the King of Ireland turned to the princess of Farafohuinn, who he was going to marry, and said "This is truly the woman I went in search of. I passed through many tests and trials for her, and I will marry none but her. Stay and celebrate with us if you wish, but otherwise you may go."

So the princess of Farafohuinn left the castle, and the Son of the King of Ireland at last married his true love.

The Black Horse

There was a king who had three sons, and when he died the youngest son was left nothing except a horse, an old, white mare with a limp. The young son realised that he would get nothing more, so he decided to leave home.

Off he went, sometimes riding the mare, sometimes walking to rest her, when he met a man riding a black horse. The two greeted each other, and the man with the black horse spoke: "I have had enough of this black beast. Will you swap him for your horse? There is one great advantage to this black horse. Wherever in the world you wish to go, he will take you there."

The king's son thought of all the places that he wished to go, and could not resist the bargain. So he exchanged his old limping horse for the stranger's mount, and went on his way.

Now the king's son had long wanted to visit the Realm Underwaves, so he decided to see if the black horse would take him. Sure enough, before the sun had risen the next day, they were there. The King Underwaves was holding court, and trying to find someone who would go to Greece, for the Prince Underwaves wanted to marry the king's daughter.

The rider of the black horse stepped forward. "Will you go to Greece to fetch the king's daughter?" asked the King Underwaves. And before he knew what he was doing, the young rider of the black horse was on his way.

As he rode, the black horse spoke to him. He explained that no one in Greece had seen a horse before, and the princess would surely want a ride. "But beware. Tell her that no man except you may ride, for some rascal may try to steal me."

When they arrived in Greece, it was just as the black horse had said. The princess saw the horse out of one of the castle windows and straight away asked for a ride. When she tried to ride the steed with her own servant, the black horse

threw the man from his back. So the princess of Greece set off
to the Realm Underwaves, and the only man to go with her
was the horse's rightful rider.

Soon they arrived in the Realm Underwaves, where the
prince was eager to arrange his wedding. But the Greek
princess spoke up. "The wedding must not be so soon," she
said. "I will not marry until I have the silver cup that my
mother used at her wedding, and her mother before her."

The Prince Underwaves turned to the rider of the black
horse. "Go back to Greece, and bring the silver cup to me
before dawn tomorrow." So the black horse and his rider set
off once more. As they travelled, the horse told his rider what
he should do. "All the king's people will be around him
tonight, and the silver cup will be passed among them. Go in
with them, pretend to be one of the people of the place, and
take the cup when it is handed to you. Then we will be away."

It all happened as the horse had said, and they were soon
back in the Realm Underwaves with the silver cup. But when
the prince began to talk of his wedding, the Greek princess
spoke up once more. "I will not marry until I have the silver
ring that my mother wore at her wedding, and her mother
before her."

The Prince Underwaves turned to the rider of the black
horse. "Go back to Greece, and bring the silver ring to me

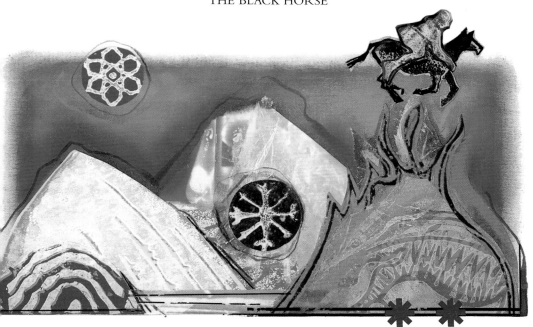

before dawn tomorrow." So the black horse and his rider set off. As they travelled, the black horse told his rider what to expect on the journey. "This is a difficult quest," said the horse. "Before we can get the ring, we will have to climb a mountain of snow, a mountain of ice, and a mountain of fire."

On they rode, and the young man was amazed at the great leaps the horse took to climb the mountains of snow and ice. Perished with cold, he clung on to the creature's mane as he made his third leap. This took them through the mountain of fire, and so fast they went that they hardly felt the heat from the flames. "Now," said the horse. "Go into that town and make an iron spike for the end of every bone in my body, and

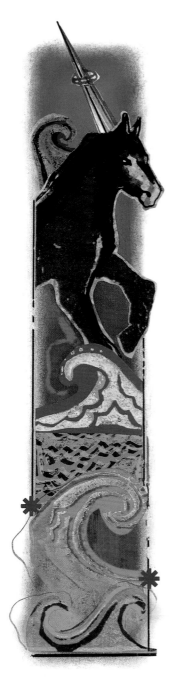

then stick the spikes into me as I tell you." The young man was puzzled, but he went to the smith and got the spikes made, and stuck them into the horse's body as he had been told.

"Near here there is a great loch," said the horse. "Watch the waters when I dive in, and you will see them covered in flames. If you see the flames go out, wait for me, and I will come to you with the ring."

The young man stood by as the horse disappeared beneath the water. Suddenly, the waters turned into bright orange flames. The young man waited and waited, but the flames still burned. He began to doubt whether he would see the black horse again. Then, just before dawn, the flames on the lake went out and the black horse appeared. There was one metal spike left, on the creature's head, and on this spike was the silver ring.

Without delay, they returned to the Realm Underwaves. Again the prince started to ask when the wedding might be,

but the princess of Greece had yet one
more demand. "I will not marry until you
build a castle for me," she said.

The Prince Underwaves looked upset.
A castle would take years to build. But the
black horse said, "This is the easiest of all
the tasks. Leave it to me." And before
long an army of diggers, stone masons,
carpenters, and metalworkers, were at
work before them, until a fine castle was
built before dawn the following day.

The rider of the black horse, the Prince
Underwaves and the princess of Greece
stood looking at the castle, which had its
own deep well. "It is a fine castle," said the
princess. "But there is still one problem
with my wedding arrangements."

"What is that?" asked the prince.

"You," said the Greek princess, and
pushed the prince into the well. "If I must
be married, then, I want to marry the
rider of the black horse, who has done
deeds of craft and valour for me while the
other man stood by."

And so it was that the young rider of the black horse married the princess of Greece, and lived in the new castle which the black horse had made for them.

Three years passed and the young rider, in his happiness, neglected the black horse. One day, as he saw the horse grazing where he had left him, the young man felt sorry for forgetting the beast that had given him so much help. "It seems as if you have someone that you prefer to me," said the horse.

"I am sorry that I forgot you," said the young man.

"It does not matter," said the horse. "Draw your sword and chop off my head, and that will be an end to it."

The young man protested,

but the horse would not take no for an answer, so the young man drew his sword and cut off the horse's head with one stroke. Straight away, the horse vanished, to be replaced by a handsome young man. "Good day to my brother-in-law," he said, and the rider of the black horse stared in puzzlement.

"You look sad to lose the horse," said the stranger. "But I hope you will be pleased to meet your brother-in-law. I was the black horse, and have been put under a spell. I used my knowledge of my father's house to help you. What is more, you kept me long and well, and, since I was put under the spell, I never met any other man who could keep me. Thank you for releasing me from the spell and giving me back my true shape." And the rider of the black horse was thankful. For now he had both a fine wife and a true friend.

The Greek Princess and the Young Gardener

There was once an old king who had one daughter. When the king grew ill it seemed as if the end of his life was coming, but he discovered that the apples from the tree in his garden made him better. So the king became angry when a strange, brightly coloured bird flew into his garden one evening and began to steal the apples.

The king called his gardener. "You are not doing your job properly!" exclaimed the king. "You must guard my apple tree day and night, for a bird is coming into the garden and stealing all the fruit."

"It will not happen again, your majesty," replied the gardener. "I will set my three sons to guard the tree. And if the bird comes near, they will shoot it with their bows and arrows."

That night, the gardener's eldest son stood guard by the apple tree. As the night went on, the boy got drowsy, and soon he was asleep at the foot of the tree. At midnight, the bird flew into the garden and removed one of the fruit. The king heard the flapping of the bird's wings, for he was a light sleeper, and dashed to his window. When he looked out, the king saw the bird taking off with one of the finest fruits in his beak. "Wake up, you lazy good-for-nothing!" he shouted at the gardener's son. The lad grabbed his bow and arrow, but by the time he had taken aim it was too late. The bird had got away.

The next night, the gardener's second son was on guard. Again the lad fell asleep and again the bird came to steal an apple. The king roared at the gardener's boy, but by the time the lad had woken, the bird had flown away again, and another of the king's finest, most succulent apples was gone from the tree. The king began to despair.

On the third evening, the gardener's youngest son stood guard. He was determined to keep awake and do himself credit with the king. As usual the bird arrived and the boy was quick enough to let loose one arrow at the bird as it flew. He did not bring the bird down, but as his arrow fell to the ground, one of the creature's feathers fell with it.

The king was pleased, for the bird had not had the chance to steal an apple before it was frightened away by the young lad's arrow. But when he saw the feather, the king was fascinated. It was made of the finest beaten gold. As he looked at it, the king decided that he wanted to catch the bird with the golden feathers. So he sent out a message. He would give half his kingdom, plus the hand of his daughter in marriage, to any man who could bring back the bird to his palace.

All the young men of the king's household, including the gardener's three sons, wondered how they could find the bird. The gardener's first son was out one day when he met a fox. "If you want to find the golden bird," said the fox, "go along

this road and take lodging
with the poor man and his
wife." So the boy went along
the road, but when he came
to the poor man's house, there
was a house opposite where
people were drinking and
dancing, and the gardener's
first son went there for his
entertainment.

The same thing happened to
the gardener's second son,
who also met the fox and was given the same advice. But the
drinking and dancing was of more interest to him, and he
joined his brother.

When the third son met the fox, the animal gave him the
same advice. Unlike his brothers, the young lad listened to
what the fox had to say, and sought lodgings with the poor
couple, and the next morning went on his way. Soon he met
the fox once more. "Well done for taking my advice," said the
fox. "Do you know where to find the golden bird?"

"I have no idea," said the young man.

"She is in the palace of the King of Spain, some two hundred
miles from here," said the fox.

The gardener's son was sad to hear that the journey was to be so long.

"Do not despair," said the fox. "Hop up on my tail, and we shall soon be there."

So off they went, and to the young gardener's surprise, they soon got to the King of Spain's palace. The fox turned to the lad again and told him where in the palace to find the golden bird. "Get the bird out as quickly as you can, and do not stay looking for other treasure," said the fox. "Then you will be safe."

The youth entered the palace and found the bird in a dull iron cage. Next to it was a fine golden cage, and the lad thought that this would be a better home for the marvellous bird. So he tried to tempt the creature into the golden cage. But all that happened was that the bird let out a terrible squeal, and the palace guards came running. Soon, the boy found himself in front of the King of Spain himself.

"I should hang you for a thief," said the king. "But I will give you a chance to win your life, and the golden bird too if you succeed. Get me the bay filly belonging to the King of Morocco, a horse that can run faster than any other. Then you shall have the golden bird."

So the young gardener found his friend the fox, and they were soon on their way to the palace of the King of Morocco.

When they arrived the fox spoke to the lad again, more sternly than before. "When you get into the stables, do not touch a thing, not even the door or the door posts. Just lead out the bay filly, and you will be fine."

But when he entered the stable, the boy saw a fine golden saddle, much better than the leather one on the filly's back, so he decided to change it over. No sooner had he touched the golden saddle than palace guards appeared from every quarter. In a few moments, the King of Morocco himself had arrived.

"I should hang you for a thief," said the king. "But there is one thing that I want, and if you can help me, then I will let you go, and the bay filly with you." And the king explained that he wanted to marry Golden Locks, the daughter of the King of Greece, and asked the gardener's boy to go to Greece and bring back the princess.

Once again, the lad and the fox set off, and again the speed of the fox was such that by nightfall they arrived at the king's palace. "Do not let her touch anything or anyone as you come out," warned the fox.

The lad found the princess and quietly explained that he wanted to take her to Morocco. At first, she was unwilling to go on such a long journey to a husband she had never met, but as she looked at the young gardener, her heart began to melt and she agreed to go with him. "Only let me kiss my father goodbye," she said. The princess went to kiss her sleeping father, promising not to waken him. But as soon as her lips touched her father's he let out a great cry, and guards came running.

When he saw that his daughter was safe, he listened to the young gardener's story. He was sad to let his daughter go, for he had already lost his son, who had been spirited away by a wicked witch. "I will only let her go if you will clear up the great heap of clay in front of my palace," said the king. For no one had been able to clear the heap before, which got larger with every shovelful of clay that was removed.

To everyone's great astonishment, including that of the young

gardener, the pile of clay was cleared. The lad knew that the fox must have had something to do with it. So the young gardener, the princess and the fox went on their way.

By the time they reached the King of Morocco's palace, the young gardener and the princess were in love. When the king brought out his bay filly to exchange for the princess, the pair looked at each other with longing. "Please let me say farewell to the princess before I depart," said the lad. While the king was distracted, the pair jumped up on the horse and rode off at top speed, the bay filly galloping faster than the wind. When they reached the King of Spain's palace, the fox was there waiting for them.

The fox turned to them before they entered the palace.

"If you give the king the filly, I will have to carry you all home, and I doubt that I have the strength. When you are about to hand over the horse, go up to the creature and stroke it, as if you are saying farewell. Then, when the king is distracted, jump on the filly's back and ride away at top speed. Then we shall return in comfort."

The king brought out the golden bird, and handed it to the gardener's boy. Instead of giving the king the filly, as he expected, the boy rode out of the palace gates, leaving the king behind him in amazement. Soon he had met up with the fox and the princess once more, and the three returned to the homeland of the young gardener.

They finally reached the spot where the lad had first met the fox, and he turned to the creature to thank him for all his help. "Now will you help me?" asked the fox. "Take your sword and chop off my head and tail." The young man could not do this to his friend, but his eldest brother, who had come to meet them, knew nothing of how the fox had helped his brother, and dealt the two blows.

The head and tail vanished, and in place of the fox was a young man. Straight away, the Greek princess recognized her brother, who had been taken away and bewitched.

If they were happy before, the Greek princess and the young gardener were now overjoyed, and they longed to share their joy with the king. So the three of them went to see the old king and his daughter, gave the king his golden bird, and told them the whole story. The Greek princess married the young gardener, and the Greek prince married the daughter of the old king. The king himself was enchanted with his golden bird. He was so pleased with the creature, he even shared with it some of the apples from his favourite tree.

Canobie Dick

Canobie Dick was a horse trader who was well known for always getting the best deal. He did not care who he did business with, so long as he got more than he paid for every piece of horse-flesh that passed through his hands.

It happened one night that Dick was riding home across Bowden Moor by the Eildon Hills. He had with him two horses that he had not been able to sell that day. As he rode he saw a figure in the distance, coming towards him. As the man got nearer, Dick saw that he was an old fellow, wearing clothes that looked positively ancient. Dick was surprised when the old man wished him good day and asked if the horses were for sale. Soon they struck a deal, and the old man paid Dick a good price in ancient gold coins. Normally Dick would have refused old coins, but he knew that gold was valuable in whatever form it came, so he took the payment readily.

A few times more Dick met the man and sold him horses, the old man always asking that Dick come at night to make the sale. When this had happened several times, Dick decided

that he should get to know
this customer better, and he
said to the man, "A bargain
is always luckier when
struck with a glass in hand."

So it was that the old man
invited Dick to his home,
but warned him, "Don't be
afraid at what you see in
my dwelling-place, for if
you do you'll be sorry for
the rest of your life."

Off they went along a
narrow path up the hills
until they came to a rocky
outcrop. To Dick's surprise,
the old man passed through
a passage into the hillside.
Although Dick had often
passed this place, he had
never noticed the passage
before.

"You are sure you are not
afraid?" said the old man.

"It is not too late to turn back."

Dick shook his head, for he did not wish to seem frightened. The passage was lit by flaming torches, and as they walked along, Dick saw a long row of stables, with a black horse in each. Next to each horse lay a knight in black armour. Nearby was an old table, and on it were a horn and a sword.

"The man that blows this horn and draws this sword shall become king of the whole of Britain," said the man.

Dick looked at the sword in fascination, lifted it briefly, but put it down again. For when he thought of the sleeping figures and the ghostly horses, he thought that drawing the sword might bring all the terrors of the mountain down upon him.

So he raised the horn to his lips and got ready to blow.

But Dick was shaking so much, and he was so breathless with fear, that all he could produce was a feeble, wavering note. Even so, this was enough to rouse the knights who were resting next to their horses. Great rumbles of thunder echoed through the rocky hall, the horses seemed to come to life and the knights rose up, their armour clanking and their swords glittering in the torch light. Once they saw the knights rise up, the horses began to neigh and stamp their hooves, tossing their heads in excitement.

The horse dealer looked at the growing army of knights and horses, coming to life around him, looking as if they were all about to launch an attack on him. Trembling, he dropped the horn, and made a grab for the great sword on the table. As he did so, a mighty voice spoke from among the knights:

> The coward shall rue the day he was born
> Who lay down the sword and blew on the horn.

As he heard these words, Dick was picked up by a mighty whirlwind that blew along the cavern and cast him out onto the open hillside. There he lay unconscious until a group of shepherds found him in the morning.

Dick told the shepherds his tale, but died soon afterwards. And no one found the passage into the hillside again.

The Knight of Riddles

Once there was a king called Ardan, king of all Albann, and his first wife died. Some time afterwards, he remarried, and the king had two sons, one from each queen. The two boys were very close, but the second queen was jealous of the king's first son, because she knew that her own boy would not inherit the kingdom. So she plotted to kill the elder son.

Twice the queen ordered her servant to put poison in the elder son's drink, and twice her own son overheard her giving the orders, and warned his brother. Then the elder son said to his brother, "I shall not live long if I stay in this house. It will be better for me if I leave home." And so the two brothers decided that they would leave together.

When they left, they took their mother's poisonous drink with them in a bottle, and before long, the eldest said, "It might not be poison after all. Let us try it on my horse." When they gave the poison to the beast, it keeled over and died.

"Well, she was a tired old nag anyway," said the elder brother. "Her time was up. Let's try the drink on your steed." So they gave the poison to the other horse, which fell down dead.

The brothers decided that at least they would skin the horse to make a blanket to keep themselves warm. While they were preparing the skin, twelve ravens flew down to feast on the carcass. But no sooner had they begun to eat than the birds fell dead from the poisoned meat.

The brothers took the dead birds with them, and when they reached the next town, they asked the baker to make twelve pies from the ravens' flesh. They packed up the pies and carried on with their journey. At night the brothers came to a dense, dark wood, and they were set upon by twenty-four robbers. "Give us your money!" demanded the thieves.

"We have no money," said the brothers. "All we have are

these meat pies."

"Food is as good as money. We will take the pies."

Greedily, the robbers began to eat the pies, and before long, they were falling down dead where they stood, for the poison was still in the meat. Relieved, the brothers went on with their journey, until they came to a fine house, which was the home of the Knight of Riddles. They decided to visit the knight, and the younger brother said that he would pretend to be the servant to the elder.

The Knight of Riddles had a beautiful daughter attended by twelve maidens. He would allow no one to marry the girl unless they could give him a riddle which he could not solve. When they heard this the brothers decided to put this riddle to him: "One killed two, and two killed twelve, and twelve killed twenty-four, and two got out of it."

The brothers stayed in the knight's house while he tried to think of an answer to the riddle, and meanwhile each of the maidens came to the younger brother and asked him what the answer to the riddle might be. They brought him gifts of cloth, but he would not tell them. "Only my brother may tell the answer," he said.

Then the knight's daughter went to the elder brother, and smiled winningly at him, and presented a gift of cloth to him, and he told her the answer to the riddle. Not long afterwards, the knight called the brothers to him and told them that he had solved the riddle.

"Your riddle was easy to solve," said the knight. "Your head will be chopped off in the morning."

"Before you behead me," said the elder brother, "I have another riddle for you. My servant and I were in the forest shooting. He shot twelve hares, skinned them, and let them go. Then came a hare finer than the rest. I shot her, skinned her, and let her go."

"That's not a difficult riddle," said the knight. And they all knew that the young man had discovered how the knight found the answers to his riddles.

The brothers had defeated the knight in their battle of the riddles, so the knight allowed the elder brother to marry his daughter. The elder prince was so full of joy that he told his brother to go home and inherit his kingdom; he would stay in the land of the Knight of the Riddles.

The elder brother did well in the country of the knight and lived there for many years. The local people were impressed at his bravery, especially when he killed three giants that were causing fear in the land. So the Knight of the Riddles gave his son-in-law his own title, the Hero of the White Shield.

The Hero of the White Shield became famed as the strongest and bravest man in the land. Many challenged him to a fight, but no one could beat the Hero. One day, a stranger came to challenge him and, after a long fight, the stranger sent the Hero jumping in alarm over a high stone wall.

"You must have some of my own fighting blood in your veins to be so strong," said the Hero of the White Shield.

"What is your family?"

"I am the son of Ardan, king of all Albann," replied the stranger. And the Hero of the White Shield knew that he had met his long-lost brother once more. The two stayed for years together in the land of the Knight of Riddles. But eventually the younger brother knew that he should return to his own kingdom, so the two parted.

On the way home, the younger brother stopped to watch twelve men playing at shinny by a tall palace. For a while he joined in, but soon the smallest of the twelve grappled with him and shook him as if he were no more than a child. "Whose sons are you, who are so strong?" he asked.

"We are the nephews of the Hero of the White Shield," they cried. And the younger brother knew that he had found his sons, and that all were alive and well. They went together to find his wife, and a great celebration was held. For hundreds of years, the kings of Albann were descended from their line.

The Humble-Bee

Two young men were out walking one summer's day and stopped by a tiny stream next to an old ruined house. They were admiring the place, and noticed how the stream turned into a miniature waterfall crossed by narrow blades of grass. One of the men was tired from the walk and the afternoon heat and sat down by the stream. Soon he was fast asleep, and the other sat quietly, watching the view.

Suddenly, a tiny creature, about the size of a humble-bee, flew out of the sleeper's mouth. It landed by the stream and crossed it by walking over some grass stalks which hung over the water at its narrowest point. The creature then approached the ruin and disappeared into one of the cracks in the wall.

The man who saw all this was shocked and decided to wake his friend to see if he was all right. As he shook his companion awake, he was astonished to see the tiny creature emerge from the ruin, fly across the stream and re-enter the sleeper's mouth, just as the young man was waking.

"What's the matter? Are you ill?" asked the watcher.

"I am well," replied the sleeper. "You have just interrupted the most wonderful dream, and I wish you had not woken me

with your shaking. I dreamed that I walked through a vast grassy plain and came to a wide river. I wanted to cross the river to see what was on the other side, and I found a place near a great waterfall where there was a bridge made of silver. I walked over the bridge and on the far bank was a beautiful palace built of stone. When I looked in, the chambers of the palace contained great mounds of gold and jewels. I was look-ing at all these fine things, wondering at the wealth of the person who left them there, and deciding which I would bring away with me. Then suddenly you woke me, and I could bring away none of the riches."

The Seal Woman

The was a farmer from Wastness who was not married. His friends used to tease him when he said he was not interested in women, but he took little notice. His only interest was his farm, which did well, and the good farmer grew rich.

One day the farmer was walking by the shore at the ebb tide, and he noticed a group of seal folk. Some were sunning themselves on a rock, others were swimming and playing in the sea. The seals were enjoying themselves and did not notice the farmer, so he crept closer and saw that they had all taken off their sealskins to reveal bodies which were as pale and white as his own.

The farmer thought what fun it would be to catch one of the naked seals, so he edged closer and then made a dash for the

seals. They grabbed their skins in alarm and jumped into the water, but the farmer managed to hold on to one of the skins.

He watched as the seals swam out to sea and then turned to walk homeward across the shore. As he went he heard a sound of sobbing behind him, and turned to see a seal-woman, weeping for her lost skin. "Oh, please give me back my skin," she cried. "I cannot join my family in the sea without it."

The farmer was filled with pity, but he was also smitten by the beauty of the seal woman, whom he thought far more attractive than any ordinary woman. So he talked to the seal woman, and told her his feelings, and soon he persuaded her to come ashore and live with him as his wife.

The seal-woman lived long with the farmer. She was as a good a farmer's wife as any normal woman, and bore him seven children, four boys and three girls. She seemed happy and people often heard her singing, but she would sometimes look with longing at the sea.

One day the farmer took his three eldest sons out in his boat to go fishing, as they often did. While they were at sea, the seal-woman sent out three of her other children to walk the shore gathering limpets and whelks. The youngest daughter stayed at home, with her mother, because the girl's foot was sore and she could not walk far.

Once they had all gone out the seal-woman started to search the house. At first she made as if she was tidying up, but her daughter realised that she was looking for something, and said to her mother, "What is it that you are looking for all around the house?"

"You must tell no one my dear," said the seal woman. "I am looking for a fine skin to make a dressing for your sore foot."

And the young girl replied, "I think I might know where you can find such a skin. One day when you were out and father thought we were asleep in bed, I saw him take a skin and look at it. Then he folded it carefully and hid it away up in the eaves above the bed."

Straight away the seal woman rushed to the place and took out the skin from under the eaves. "Farewell my little one," she said as she rushed out of the door and ran in the direction of the shore. There she put on her skin, dived into the sea, and swam quickly away. A male seal saw her coming and greeted her with excitement, for he recognized the seal he had loved

long ago.

As the farmer was returning to shore in his boat, he saw his wife diving into the sea and making for the male seal. "Farewell, dear husband," she called to him. "I liked you well and you treated me kindly. But it is time that I returned to my true love of the sea."

That was the last the farmer saw of the seal woman. He missed his seal-wife greatly, and it took him many years to recover from his sadness. And he often went for walks along the shore, hoping to catch sight of her again.

Rashen Coatie

There was a king whose queen died young, and after a time he remarried. His new queen was a widow, and both king and queen had a daughter from their first marriage. The king's daughter, Rashen Coatie, was good and beautiful, while the daughter of the queen was ill-featured and bad-tempered.

The queen treated the king's daughter badly in the hope that her own girl would gain. Her husband, anxious to keep the peace at home, turned a blind eye to this ill-treatment, and so it came about that Rashen Coatie ended up looking after the king's cattle, while the queen's daughter stayed at home and wallowed in luxury.

Every day the queen sent her own daughter with the worst food for Rashen Coatie to eat, in the hope that the girl would fall ill and die. But Rashen Coatie met a fairy, who taught her a spell. Whenever the girl said the magic words, a calf appeared, bringing her food as fine as any that was eaten in the king's palace. In this way, Rashen Coatie became stronger and more beautiful than ever, and the queen became angrier and angrier.

When it was clear that her plan was failing, the queen went to talk to a witch. The witch gave the queen the power to look into the unknown, and the envious woman quickly realised that it was the calf who was giving Rashen Coatie her food.

Straight away she went to her husband and asked him to have the calf killed, so that she might cook the animal for a banquet, and the king agreed. Rashen Coatie was distressed when she heard what was to happen, but the calf came to her and spoke in her ear. "If you do what I say you need not worry," said the calf. "When I am cooked and eaten, take my bones and bury them under this stone. Do this, and leave the palace

for a while, and you will be safe."

Rashen Coatie buried the bones beneath the stone, left the palace, and went into hiding. The calf came back to life and brought her food and so she was able to survive. Meanwhile, the queen was poisoned when she ate the calf's entrails and, after a long illness, finally died.

By this time, Rashen Coatie was grown into a fine young woman. She did not know how well she would be received at her father's court, so decided to return in disguise. But when she arrived she was thrown into confusion. Her father was so taken with her beauty that he wanted to marry her. She ran to the calf to ask him what to do.

"Ask the king for clothes made of the rushes that grow by the stream," said the calf. The king had just such a dress made, and still he wanted to marry Rashen Coatie.

"Ask the king for a dress of all the colours of the birds of the air," said the calf. The king gave her a dress with all the colours of the birds of the air, and still he wanted to marry her.

"Ask the king for a dress, with the colours of all the fish of the sea," said the calf. But again the king produced just such a dress, and still he wanted to marry Rashen Coatie.

So finally the girl felt she had used up all the possible excuses to delay, and the wedding day arrived. When she got to church, Rashen Coatie tried one last objection. "I must have

the ring my mother wore when she was married," she said.
And then she put on her dress of rushes, and ran from her
father's kingdom.

  After long wandering, Rashen Coatie came to a hunting
lodge which belonged to a prince. No one seemed to be there,
so exhausted, she collapsed on to the prince's bed, and fell into
a deep sleep. Later, the prince himself arrived and found
Rashen Coatie asleep on his bed. He woke the girl and asked
what she was doing there. "I meant no harm," she said. "I am
far from home and was tired and lost. Is there some place near
here where I might find work?" So the prince took Rashen
Coatie home and she was put to work in the palace kitchens.

Soon it was Christmas and all the people in the palace, from the prince to his lowliest servants, went to church in the morning. Only Rashen Coatie was left in the kitchen to turn the roasting spits.

She too wanted to go to church, and decided to use a spell the calf had taught her so the spits would turn themselves:

> Every spit turn on your way
> Until I return on this yule day.

And with that, Rashen Coatie put on her finest dress and ran off to church.

In church, the prince was entranced by the beautiful young

woman who entered just as the service was beginning. Little did he guess that it was the kitchen maid Rashen Coatie. The prince decided to speak to her as she left the church, but she slipped out quickly and ran back to the palace, hoping that none would know that she had left the kitchen.

But as the girl flew along the path, one of her tiny golden shoes came off and she left it behind in her haste. The prince knew now what he should do. "The woman whose foot fits this shoe shall be my bride," he said.

Hundreds of women came to the palace, but no foot fitted the shoe perfectly. Then the witch's daughter appeared, and she had pared her nails and even rubbed some of the skin off her heels, so that she could squeeze on the shoe. The prince knew that she was not the woman he had seen, but he was true to his word, and announced that he would marry the girl. But a small bird fluttered over the prince's head, singing:

> Clipped the heel and pared the toe;
> In the kitchen the shoe will go.

The prince turned back and ran to the kitchen, finding Rashen Coatie, who had not tried on the shoe. When it fitted, the prince went to church with his rightful bride.

The fairy tales of Scotland portray a world of magic and shape-changing. Horses and foxes that turn into handsome princes, a seal who is also a woman, thorns that turn into woods and a tiny stone that becomes an enormous rock – these are some of the amazing transformations that take place in these stories.

This book contains some of the best and most gripping of Scotland's traditional tales. Their characters, from jealous stepmothers and gruesome ghosts to chivalrous princes and beautiful princesses, are some of the most memorable in all folk literature, and their stories range in mood from the amusing to the touching. Superbly illustrated by five top illustrators, *Scottish Fairy Tales* will delight young and old alike.